THE CONTESTS
AT COWLICK

Weekly Reader Books presents

THE CONTESTS AT COWLICK

by
Richard Kennedy
illustrated by
Marc Simont

An Atlantic Monthly Press Book
Little, Brown and Company
BOSTON   TORONTO

Books by Richard Kennedy

THE PARROT AND THE THIEF
THE CONTESTS AT COWLICK

This book is a presentation of
Weekly Reader Books.
Weekly Reader Books offers book clubs for children
from preschool through junior high school.
All quality hardcover books are selected by
a distinguished Weekly Reader Selection Board.
For further information write to:
Weekly Reader Books
1250 Fairwood Ave.
Columbus, Ohio 43216

COPYRIGHT © 1975 BY RICHARD KENNEDY

ILLUSTRATIONS COPYRIGHT © 1975 BY MARC SIMONT

Library of Congress Cataloging in Publication Data

Kennedy, Richard
  The contests at Cowlick.

  "An Atlantic-Monthly Press book."
  SUMMARY: Wally outwits a gang of outlaws
and saves the town of Cowlick.
  [1. Western stories.   2.   Humorous stories]
I.   Simont, Marc, ill.   II.   Title.
PZ7.K385Co   [Fic]   74-23566
ISBN 0-316-48863-1

ATLANTIC-LITTLE, BROWN BOOKS
ARE PUBLISHED BY
LITTLE, BROWN AND COMPANY
IN ASSOCIATION WITH
THE ATLANTIC MONTHLY PRESS

*Published simultaneously in Canada
by Little, Brown & Company (Canada) Limited*

PRINTED IN THE UNITED STATES OF AMERICA

For Joseph and for Matthew

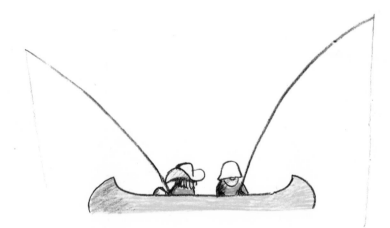

Hogbone and his gang rode into the little town of Cowlick one dusty afternoon when the sheriff and his men had gone fishing.

"If you need us," the sheriff said as they left, "we'll just be a holler up the creek."

So when the townsfolk saw Hogbone
and his gang coming they hollered for
the sheriff and his men. First the mayor
hollered.

Then the baker. Then the barber.

Then several others tried it, and the banker hollered loudest of all. But when the sheriff and his men did not come, the townsfolk ran off to hide.

The streets were empty, doors latched, and windows locked as Hogbone and his gang rode up the main street. Here and there an eyeball showed at a knothole or between boards, and shadows moved with cat slowness behind curtains.

Hogbone and his fifteen men pulled up their horses in front of the bank. For the looks of it, Cowlick might have been a ghost town.

"Hey!" Hogbone yelled out, "where's all the chickens in this coop? Hah?—how about it? Where's your sissy sheriff and his girl friends? Bring 'em out so we can shoot 'em for a while!"

The shadows froze on the curtains, and not an eyeball showed.

"Well, shucks! This ain't no fun," Hogbone complained. "Heck! Well, go git the money, boys." Scratching and spitting, some of the men got down off their horses. "Heck!" Hogbone said again, "I was looking for a little trouble."

At this moment Wally crawled out from under a horse trough and stood before the Hogbone gang.

"If you want some trouble," said Wally, "I can give you some trouble."

Hogbone dropped a look on the boy
and said, "Most trouble you'd give me
is sticken' between my teeth when I
chaw you up."

"Har, har, har!" laughed the gang.

"Shut up!" said Hogbone.

"I'm the fastest runner anywhere around here," said Wally. "I bet I can win a footrace with your five best men."

"Well, ain't that a pretty how-de-do? I just reckon we might use a little fun." And Hogbone called out, "Alligator, Blackwhip, Snakebite, Gouge-eye, Crumby—git down here and do a little leg-stretching."

The men got down off their horses and Wally drew a line in the dust.

"We'll race down to the end of the street, around the corner and into McGee's Livery Stable," said Wally, getting down on the line. The five men hitched up their pants and kicked their spurs off, sailed their hats out of the way and dropped their gun belts. They hunched down on the line with Wally.

"Ready?" Wally said.

"Ready," the men grunted.

Hogbone held up his forty-four. "On your marks—get set—" BLAM!

The runners jolted across the line. Wally ran last—all the way down the street, and he was the last one around the corner. Some townsfolk came out of hiding as the runners raced by.

When Wally got to McGee's Livery
Stable all five men were inside,
laughing at him as he jogged up to the
door. Wally smiled and slammed the
heavy door on them and bolted it shut.
He walked slowly back to Hogbone

and the remaining ten men of the gang.
A few more townsfolk were standing
timidly about on the dusty street.

"They beat me," said Wally. "They
got a drink and sprawled out in the
straw."

"Har, har!" laughed Hogbone.

"Har, har, har!" laughed his men.

"Shut up!" growled Hogbone.

"I got a bad start or I could
have beat them," Wally said. "So that
didn't count much. But I'll give you
another try. Pick five men and I bet I

can climb faster than any of them."

"You're a sassy little mouse," said
Hogbone. "What you need is a good
whupping, and I got the men to do it."
And he called out, "Horseblanket,
Saddlehorn, Cinch, Rakespur, Yankbit,
git over here!"

The five men got over there, grinning as they dropped their gun belts, took off their spurs and tucked at their shirts. More townsfolk came out to watch.

"We'll need two long ladders set up against the side of the church," said Wally. Some big boys ran off and got two twenty-foot ladders and set them up. Everyone stood around as Wally called out the rules of the contest. "Now, you five men go up that ladder and I go up the other one, and I mean to beat you all to the top and sit on the roof of the church first."

"This ought to be good," said Hogbone. "We might even have a

neck-breaking." And he raised his forty-four.

BLAM!

The climbers jumped at their ladders and clambered up.

All five men were up and across the roof and sitting on the ridgepole of the church before Wally was even at the top of his ladder. He stopped climbing and looked down. More townsfolk had come out of hiding to watch the contests. Some were carrying guns.

"Darn!" said Wally, looking up to the men on the roof above him. "You guys sure are good climbers."

"You ain't bad yourself for a sprout," said Horseblanket.

Wally yelled down to Hogbone.
"They beat me fair, but I got one other
contest I know I can beat those last five
men at."

"Come on down off there ya little

rooster and I'll give you a last chance," Hogbone yelled back.

Wally turned to the men on the roof again. "I'll bet you guys could outclimb a mountain goat."

"Ain't bad yourself, for a kid," said Saddlehorn.

"You guys comfortable up there?

Can you see pretty good?" Wally
asked.

"Just fine," said Rakespur.

"Best seat in the house," said
Yankbit.

"It's a cinch," said Cinch.

So Wally left them on the roof and
climbed down. By now there was a
good crowd of townsfolk standing
around.

"I know I don't look so strong," said
Wally to Hogbone.

"Ya look like my little bitty sister,"
said Hogbone.

"Maybe so," Wally said, "but I can
lift my horse over there." He pointed to
a small pinto tied to a rail.

"I gotta see that," said Hogbone, "even if he is a runt horse."

"Okay," Wally said, "then it's a contest. I bet you I can lift my horse and I bet your five men there can't lift those big pigs they're riding."

Hogbone got red in the face and yelled, "Bump, Stump, Crump, Dump, Lump—git over here with your big—with your horses!" The men gathered around with their horses and Wally brought his pinto over.

"Now if you never lifted a horse before I can tell you it's a bit tricky," said Wally. "You have to get right underneath and lift straight up. Trouble is, the horse wants to slide off

your back. So what you have to do is tie him on real tight. Here, get underneath your horses and I'll show you how it's done. Some of you people give a hand here," he said to the townsfolk.

Wally took a lasso from Bump's horse and tied it around over the top of the saddle and around under Bump's belly, and he took several loops like that and knotted the rope tight.

"That's how it's done," said Wally. The other men were tied under their horses the same way, tight up so just their feet and the tips of their fingers touched the ground.

"You sure got some pretty funny
ideas," said Hogbone, studying the
men under their horses.

"Pretty funny," said Wally. Then he

walked over to the church and pulled both ladders away, and they slammed to the ground.

"Hey!" Yankbit shouted from the roof. "How we gonna git down from here?"

Right about then Hogbone began to catch on. He looked down the street where his runners had disappeared, then to the men on the roof, and then to the men tied underneath their own horses. He took out his forty-four and pointed it right between Wally's eyes. The townsfolk began to catch on, too, and a couple of the men pointed their rifles at Hogbone.

Wally spoke: "Now five of your men
are locked in McGee's Livery Stable,

and five are stuck on the church roof,

and five are tied underneath their horses, and it looks like you can't do much alone."

"I can blow your head off," snarled
Hogbone.

"Won't do you any good," said
Wally, looking toward the men with
rifles. "My friends here won't like that.

Besides, you can have your men back
and all the money in the bank if you
can holler louder than me."

"Har, har!" laughed Hogbone. "A hollering contest? You think I got to be boss of this gang for nothing?"

"Har, har, har!" laughed his men.

"Shut up!" shouted Hogbone. The men shut up.

"You holler first," said Wally.

Hogbone scratched his chin and looked around very carefully. Then he shrugged and stuck his gun away in his holster.

"Okay," he said, "give me some air-sucking room." He spread his arms out and everyone moved back. Then he took a great breath of air and let out a holler.

"WHOOOOOOOOOOOOOOOOO OOOOOOAAAAAAAAAAAAA!"

"Pretty good," said Wally, "but I can holler louder. You've got to bring it way up from deep in the stomach."

"You think I don't know that?" said Hogbone. "Listen."

"YOWWWWWWWWWWWWWW WWWWWWWWWWWWWWWW OOOOOOOOOOOOOOO!"

"Not bad," said Wally, "but I can do better. If you took off your gun belt you could get more wind."

"That's a fact," agreed Hogbone, and he dropped his gun belt aside.

"HAAAAAAAAAAAAAAAA AAAAAAAAAAAAAAAEEEE EEEEEEEEEEEEEYYYYY YYYYYY!"

"Take off your hat and toss your
head back more," Wally suggested.

On his sixth try, Hogbone's hollers
were still improving. On his seventh
try the sheriff and his men, who had
been just a holler up the creek, rode up

quietly behind Hogbone and took him by the arms. Hogbone was so winded from hollering that he didn't even put up a fight when the sheriff hauled him off. The rest of the gang were rounded up and clapped in jail with him.

As Wally passed the jail window
Hogbone glared out at him.

"Pretty funny," Hogbone snarled.

"Har, har, har!" laughed his men.

"Shut up!" said Hogbone.

Then Wally got together his fishing
gear and headed up the creek.